A FATHER CHRISTMAS STORY

Being

A Tale of How Father Christmas Came to Be

A FATHER CHRISTMAS STORY

Being

A Tale of How Father Christmas Came to Be

by

Paul T Kidd

Cheshire Henbury

First published in 2007 by Cheshire Henbury
ISBN 978-1-901864-09-0

British Library Cataloguing in Publication Data.
A catalogue record for this book is available from the British Library.

Cheshire Henbury
E-mail:
books@cheshirehenbury.com

Web site:
http://www.cheshirehenbury.com/afatherchristmasstory

Printed and bound by CPI Antony Rowe, Eastbourne

To Judith, Lucy, Tara and Dale

PREFACE

It is Christmas Eve. The snow is gently falling outside. White is the surrounding countryside and within, all is snug and warm. Gathered around a blazing fire, everyone is content and full of expectation for the excitement of the coming morning, with all its surprises and delights. Then someone among those assembled asks, "Where did the tale of Father Christmas came from?" They want to know the origins of the story of a man dressed in red and full of good cheer, driving reindeer across the starry skies, delivering gifts to every child. However, dear reader, this is a question posed by the enquiring logical mind, seeking to know the world as it is. Alas it is the wrong one to ask.

Father Christmas is a precious gift of the imagination, a link to childhood, and on Christmas Eve, when the waiting world is full of anticipation, it is far better to allow fantasy to take hold. So in answer to the question just posed, I say in return, where do you want the tale to come from?

In this little book I have provided an answer in keeping with the Christmas season, one that will awaken the Christmas spirit even in the most cynical, one that I think will please all, regardless of age, and I hope one that will add to your Christmas cheer. The story is primarily aimed at adults, but it can be read aloud to younger children. Now read on, and in doing so, allow yourself, for a brief moment, to revisit the enchantment, the thrill, and the sense of mystery that is so much apart of every child's Christmas Eve.

Paul T Kidd
December 2006

CONTENTS

A FATHER CHRISTMAS STORY

CHAPTER ONE

JOURNEY INTO THE FOREST

There was an age, long distant now, when there was no Father Christmas! With respect to this there is no doubt for it is a historical fact. Imagine that, no Father Christmas! Then it all began, one Yuletide Eve, long, long ago in a far away place, deep inside the frozen lands of the north, close to where the vast coniferous forests that are the habitat of the wild brown bear, gives way to the treeless domain of the great white bear. There, in a time before time, before the world was full of clocks that measure the slipping away of every fleeting second, before there were any calendars to reckon the passing of the days, when there was no need for such things, and the passage of time was noted by the turning of the seasons, extraordinary events did unfold. There, in this now distant and long forgotten world, Father Christmas made his first appearance and the magic of Christmas began.

How did this happen? What tale is there to tell? What story?

In answer I say, quite an amazing one, but the telling of it has long since ceased to be a tradition. Much of the fable that is the story of Father Christmas has now largely been forgotten, lost to the modern world, caught up as it is in living for the moment in an endless quest for instant gratification. But not forgotten by all! For there are those that hold on to such things, preserving the details so that the knowledge is not forever lost. Now, how this information came to me is a tale in its own right, and one that will have to wait another time for its telling. On this matter that is all I will say. But of the story that is for the telling, this started innocuously, on a winter's night that could have been like any other, only it was not!

~

Like a frozen blanket the freezing night air wrapped itself around Nicholas as soon as he stepped out that Yuletide Eve—it was the embrace of death, but only for the novice or the fool. For those who, like Nicholas, lived every long winter's day with this peril, and knew how to cope, how to avoid the dangers, it was just one more extremely cold night—the sort that chills to the bone in a matter of seconds.

No more gentle a person, no more warm a soul, no more kindly a spirit could this determined enemy try to clasp within its deathly claws.

"Too soft, Nicholas," his Father had often said, when, as Nicholas had been inclined to do as a small boy, he had rescued yet another helpless wild creature that had fallen fowl of the deadly world of snow and ice. But Nicholas did not think himself too soft, for it was compassion for all living things that had driven Nicholas to so behave when young, and it was an endearing characteristic that had not faded with the passage of time. He still practised this, and was always concerned for the wild animals that lived in the woods, constantly alert to any that may be in need of his assistance. Now, as an adult, this distinguishing feature of his personality was to influence his future in a way that neither he, nor his Father, nor any of his dear and close friends could have ever predicted.

But before I reveal why this is so, it is necessary to tell you about the climatic conditions that year, for these too had a bearing on events that night. Both personality and weather, taken together, combined to create a set of circumstances that led to the outcome of this tale, taking in some peculiar encounters on the way, and ending with … Be patient, I will, in due course, reveal all.

Now, to return to the matter of the weather, for without doubt this was an important determining element in what took place that Yuletide Eve.

The cold season had come early. It was autumn when the first snow fell, like a white sheet cast across the northern parts of the world, in an instant transforming the landscape into a vast snowy desert.

Snow in autumn was bad news for those who dwelt in the sub Arctic. The early arrival of whiteness was usually a sign that the winter would be colder and longer than usual. This was not a welcome prospect in a region with short summers. Indeed, the summer just gone, when the sun had reached its highest position in its never-ending daily trek across the sky, had been a fairly poor one. So the prospect of an even colder winter than normal, following on from a half-hearted summer, was not a pleasant thought for the hardy inhabitants of those realms.

This is how that winter turned out. A harsher one no-one could recall. This increased the hardships which Nicholas and others like him had to endure. All suffered that year, both man and beast. Food was in short supply, and the wild life, at least those creatures that did not sleep through the season, went hungry. For the men who worked in the vast forest, who eked out a meagre existence in a land that was at the best of times a difficult place to dwell, life had become even more arduous than is common during the long cold winter months.

Nicholas was one of these hard-working woodsmen, living off the land, using the timber, nature's bountiful crop, to earn a living as best he could.

No-one owned the wild wood. The forest belonged to all. From its centre it spread in every direction for hundreds of kilometres, and if one could look down on it from high above, it would, for all appearances, seem as if some giant hand had laid-out a dark green belt across the lands just below the Arctic. Only in winter, most of what should have been green was white.

The forest was a habitat where many animals, some quite fierce and dangerous, found shelter and food. It was also a place where humankind exploited the Earth's resources, as they are inclined to do, using these to fashion for themselves a different existence, not wholly constrained by the environment, but still governed by the climate's eternally shifting moods.

Nicholas was not concerned about the cold for he understood the weather—its power, its temperament—and he was well protected with suitable warm garments. He wore a tunic consisting of several layers of fur stitched together to keep him warm. His trousers, his large brown snow boots, his thick cloves, and his hat—all these were lined with soft warm fur. Above all this protection he was attired in a magnificent long green hooded cloak, trimmed along the edges with the fur of the white fox. Wearing this he looked very grand—almost regal. This however was not its purpose. Its primary function was to keep out the biting wind. In that land of snow and ice the wind was a merciless enemy. It could easily cut through several layers of clothing, bringing with it hypothermia and the end of life for those who fell within its deadly clutches. The locals called this the sleeping death.

In Nicholas' frozen world, all was covered in deep virgin white snow—there being little pollution in those far off times to contaminate and corrupt the pristine whiteness. Here and there loose powdery snow was piled up in high drifts, blown there by the icy polar winds. With the winter being harder than normal, with heavy falls of snow lying deeper on the ground than was typical, these drifts were much higher than he or anyone else, had previously seen.

Polar winds were an ever-present danger in Nicholas' life during the cold season. When they blew down from the polar ice cap they turned falling snow, and that which lay loose on the ground, into raging blizzards—transforming the world into a swirling white maelstrom. It was a deadly mixture for anyone unfortunate to be caught up in such weather. Bitingly cold and potentially lethal they were, but for those who lived in the most northerly inhabited parts of the globe, the polar winds were just another hazardous feature of their isolated world.

Nicholas knew immediately that that winter's night was different from the many others he had experienced.

"Um! What's this?" he thought. "What's going on out there?"

There was an aspect to that night which was mysterious, extraordinary, and strangely enchanting, and he sensed this. The unusual atmosphere seemed to hang over the snow-clad landscape, permeating every frozen nook and cranny. The feeling, the sensation, was one of wonder not of fear, but its cause he did he know. But this he was destined to discover, and soon.

Nicholas' mindfulness came from long practice of reading nature's signs. Call it sixth sense if you will, but these perceptions of the ambience were a skill that came from living life in close harmony with the environment, respecting the unpredictability of the weather, and understanding the peculiarities of its ways.

So, for a brief moment Nicholas hesitated, as if suspended between the warmth and cosiness of his home and the cold, white, and snowy world that lay beyond. He stood on his veranda, not sure whether to proceed or to go back indoors.

"Perhaps I should leave this till the morning, when it's light," he thought.

This was one of those many instants that happen every day, junctures that have the potential to become life changing—the *if only* moments, in which, with the benefit of hindsight, one would probably have taken a different decision. It is also true however that these decision points, these few seconds, when what seem like simple choices present themselves, and decisions are made, these are the times when one's destiny is shaped, for better or worse. Not to step forward in such circumstances, to stay within the safety of the familiar and the comfortable, is not to live at all, for life is risk and to take no risk is as though to forfeit life, yet to take risk sometimes leads to the same result, but in a different sense.

A quiet voice inside Nicholas' mind was telling him that it was all right to continue with his plans. This was his intuition at work and he was inclined to take note of this for it had served him well in the past.

"It'll be fine," he said to himself aloud.

Living alone in such a climate meant that he not only had a rapport with the environment, but that he was also more in tune with his inner self than most, especially those who lived in larger settlements, more cut off from the close encounter with the immense and powerful creature called nature which was so much a part of Nicholas' life. So the decision was taken—he would make the journey. It was a fateful choice.

The air was crystal clear. There was a sharp frost and the raw cold was nipping at his nose.

"I'll need more seal oil on my face," he thought. He knew this immediately he felt the cold—that determined foe—attacking his exposed skin.

High above in the starry heavens tiny specs of light twinkled in the crisp night air—the small effects, seen in this world, of incomprehensible and enormous events taking place in millions of far distant celestial bodies. Together these points of light, set against the inky blackness of the night sky, formed patterns that were familiar to Nicholas.

He had spent many long nights gazing up at the stars in wonderment at the pictures that formed in the minds of those familiar with the stars' positions relative to one another. There was the Great Bear. This was present right throughout the long year, but not easily seen at the height of summer, when the sun seemed to sit below the horizon, just out of sight, lighting up the land, illuminating the night sky and keeping the full darkness at bay. In winter there was the Great Hunter, striding across the wintry skyline above the forest, keeping watch over the sleeping world below. These were just two of the many constellations that his people had given names to, but there were many more that went unnamed, familiar patterns, steadfast and unchanging, like the great forest, forming the back-cloth to his life.

Nicholas lived in an old wooden house at the edge of the large forest that occupied an appreciable portion of the cold northern regions. His dwelling consisted of a two-story structure, with a cellar, and several attached outbuildings. In one of these he kept his team of eight reindeer along with his snow sleigh. These he would be using on his journey that night.

North of the house stretched the vast tundra where no trees grew, leading eventually to the polar regions, with vast stretches of frozen sea ice, a place where enormous white bears patrolled a still, white, barren world, seeking out the prey that would sustain them in that inhospitable habitat. Nicholas had seen these creatures for himself, for in the summer season, when the ice retreated, they sometimes came south looking for food. He was wary of these great white bears for they had a fearsome reputation.

South of Nicholas' home lay the dark forest that sustained his way of life, for he, being a woodsman, used these trees, which were mostly spruce and firs, to provide himself with wood of all shapes and sizes. Some of this timber he sold to people living in the several settlements that lay within a day's journey of his abode. From this trade he made his livelihood, providing the income that he needed to purchase those items that he could not grow or make for himself. It was towards the trees that Nicholas intended to head upon that special night, into the immense and dark forest with all its surprises and its hidden dangers.

The purpose of his journeying out on such a harsh winter's evening was to bring home a Yule Log for his fire. It was a task that should have been done already. The job had not been completed because it had been a busy year, and with the early onset of winter, which had slowed down his work, he had not found time until that night, to haul it from the forest, to his home. Thus it was that if it had not been for the weather, for the arrival of snow before it was due, he would that night not have left the comfort of his home, and all that followed would not have happened.

His Yule Log had already been cut and lay in the forest awaiting collection. It was a section of spruce tree that he had felled earlier during the autumn. Every year for as long as he could recall, he had identified a dead tree, chopped it down, and then cut from it a large section of trunk, big enough to burn in his fire for the full twelve days of Yuletide. His father, and his father before him, and so on back across the generations of his ancestors, had done the same task at that time of year. It was an age-old tradition in those parts and one that Nicholas was happy to continue. Being part of his existence, the ritual was a constituent of the annual cycle of life, one of the many yearly activities that served to highlight the passing of time and the turning of the seasons.

Mid-winter was a bleak and dismal time of year and Nicholas was eager to make the season as cheerful as he could, this being he believed, the main reason for having a Yuletide celebration. A large section of spruce tree, burning day and night in the fireplace, would be a welcome relief from the monotony of long dark nights and short dull winter days.

Nicholas, like the rest of the region's population, scattered across the land in small settlements and isolated dwellings, would create for a short time, a bright and welcoming sight. This he would enjoy by staying home as much as possible and making the most of the decorations and other delights that he had prepared. For in addition to burning the Yule Log, Nicholas, like everyone else, had bedecked his dwelling with ivy, mistletoe, and with holly branches heavily laden with bright red berries. Garlands of bushy green spruce branches were strung around his rooms, and he had placed small oil lamps in his windows that would burn day and night for the twelve days of Yuletide. These would light up his home for anyone who passed by to see.

Above all Nicholas would partake in a feast of food, including roasted reindeer and wild goose, which would be served with pickled vegetables and preserved fruits that had been prepared during the summer season when the earth was soft and when wild and cultivated plants yielded their rich harvest. Best of all, there would be sweet pies and puddings made from exotic dried fruits imported into the region from far distant warmer realms.

On the whole it was a lonely existence for Nicholas, but not one entirely devoid of company. Often he was visited by nomadic reindeer herders, who, in exchange for a few nights accommodation in Nicholas' home, provided him with supplies of reindeer meat and hides. Fellow woodsmen were also frequent visitors, as he was to them, and there were regular outings to the nearby settlement that lay ten kilometres away, where he bought his supplies.

Now although Nicholas would be staying at home for most of Yuletide, he would not be spending the whole time on his own. He had arranged for friends to come over the following morning to share with him the food that he had prepared. He had also made small gifts for them, as was the tradition, and he had been asked by a number of his friends to come to their homes as well. So taken altogether there would be time for both solitude and socialising, and the balance for Nicholas was about right.

Standing on the south-facing veranda outside his front door, with the cold frosty air gnawing away at his nose, Nicholas cast his eyes over the scene that lay before him. The moon was rising in the east, now its crescent phase and past it best as a light source, waning as every day passed, it still provided enough illumination to lift slightly the veil of darkness that the night had brought. The blanket of snow that had descended on the landscape over two months back, created sufficient reflected light for Nicholas to navigate his way along the forest tracks without danger of running off the roads or colliding with rocks by the wayside.

He stepped forward on to the snow, now well compacted in the area in front of his dwelling. Heavy as the frost was, it went largely unnoticed in a world that was already almost entirely white and frozen. Behind him, in the northern sky, there was the usual display of dancing lights, changing colour from green to blue and flickering like a candle flame caught in a gentle breeze.

Although it was winter, the forest of spruces and firs that stretched into the far distance—south, east, and west—was alive with creatures of the night. Hungry wolves prowled the woods, and they howled in the distance, their lament travelling far and wide through the still air, and that night, for some unknown reason, they seemed to be more vocal than normal.

"The wolves are agitated," Nicholas thought. "There's definitely something out there that's not right tonight. But what?"

Wolves did not usually worry Nicholas too much, although

he did respect them, and was wise enough to fear them. He had lived all his life in that harsh cold environment, and knew how to survive amidst all the dangers that surrounded him, and that included how to deal with wolves. So he was use to them and knew how to keep them at bay.

His wilderness skills he had learnt as a boy from his Father and Grandfather. He hoped one day to pass these on to another generation, but to do that he would first need to find a wife, and with that aim he was making some progress, for not so far away lived a woman whom he liked very much. She was also attracted to Nicholas and he spent as much time with her as he could—she would be one of the friends he would be visiting over the Yuletide period.

Now Nicholas being a gentleperson liked the idea of being a father. He often made wooden toys for the offspring of his friends, and he was well liked by all children. They, it seemed, knew of some talent, some gift, that was not so obvious to adults, and he was always a welcome guest in any home where there were little ones.

Nicholas strode over to the barn to his left, to the place where he kept his reindeer and his snow sleigh. On entering he was greeted by the pungent smell of reindeer droppings. Although his animals were hardy and use to the cold, he liked to keep them warm during the winter and he kept a small wood burning stove constantly lit in the barn to keep the frost at bay. So inside it was warm, but this meant that it was also slightly smelly. Nicholas could have created more ventilation, which would have helped to clear the atmosphere, but it would also have let in the chilly air, and he did not want to do that. His reindeer were precious to him, and he treated them kindly, regularly tending to their needs, ensuring that they were properly fed, exercised, and he never overworked them. This was not just a matter of kindness to his animals, but also a practical matter. Nicholas knew that on nights such as that one, his safety, his life, depended upon his reindeer being fit and healthy—he could not afford for any of them to fail him out in the snowy world into which he was about to head.

The snow sleigh was a sight to behold. It was no simple crude sledge of the type that most woodsmen used to haul timber during the winter months. No, this was a fine ornate piece of craftsmanship dating back several generations, and it was made for transporting people and their luggage. There were front, side and rear panels that kept passengers safe, both from falling off the sledge, but also from the dangers that often lurked at roadsides, such as wild animals or protruding branches. Each of these panels was coloured bright red and decorated with symbols such as trees, fruits, and animals, all painted in lucid colours such as green, yellow and blue, contrasting sharply with the bright red background. The panels bulged slightly to the outside, creating more space within. There were four seats, each with backrests, in the sleigh, arranged in pairs, in two rows, and each was covered with reindeer hide, and at the back there was space for luggage and other such items.

The rear and side panels were higher than the front one and in the forward part of each side panel there was a lockable door that provided access to the sleigh. The tops of these side panels were finished with carved and curved wooden strips that swept upwards from front to back, curving back on themselves towards the rear, so that from a side view the panels looked like large waves about to break upon some far distant shore. The body of the sleigh was mounted on strong metal runners that enabled the sleigh to effortlessly glide across snow and ice. Kept inside the sleigh was an ample supply of furs to keep passengers warm as they moved on their way through the cold sharp air.

Mounted on each of the four-corners were oil lamps.

"Now to light the oil lamps," Nicholas said aloud, knowing that his reindeer liked to hear his reassuring voice.

As he lit the lamps he checked that each was full with oil.

"Where's that supply of extra oil?" he asked himself. "Ah there it is, safe and secure in its usual place."

Oil lamps alone however were not enough to keep desperate wolves at bay. So in addition to these lamps, there were also fitted at each of the four-corners of the sleigh, blazing torches that were positioned atop of the lamps. These burnt fiercely once lit, they being made of oiled cloth wrapped around a wooden shaft, and protected affront by a metal shield which kept them from being extinguished by the onrush of air as the sleigh moved across the frozen land. The wolves did not care for these flaming beacons burning brightly in the darkness, and they kept well away when they were lit. Nicholas kept four spare torches onboard in case any should burn out during a journey.

The reindeer were restless that night, sensing, like Nicholas, that there was a special aspect to the evening, and that all was not normal. Animals have this sense—they know when there is a change, or when danger is present.

Understanding his reindeer, Nicholas knew that it was necessary to reassure the animals, so, as he placed leather harnesses on to each of the eight animals, he spoke to them.

"Easy my friends," he said in a gentle but firm voice, stroking their necks and backs as he did so. "Easy my friends, nothing to worry about. All is well. Nothing to fear on this night."

After completing this task Nicholas then led them, one at a time, to the sleigh. Attached to each harness was a small bell, which softly jingled with every movement of the reindeer. Hitching each of the creatures to the system of ropes and straps that would keep them in their positions connected together, and to the sleigh, he was soon ready for departure.

"Ya!" Nicholas said gently, after climbing aboard the sleigh. The team of reindeer slowly moved forward in unison, out of the stable into the coldness of the night air. Once again Nicholas felt the bitter cold hit him in the face as soon as he passed through the doorway. It was as if he were moving through an invisible curtain—one moment there was relative warmth, the next, sharp, biting, tingling sensations on the skin. It was a feature of life that Nicholas had never fully become accustomed to, and although his face had become hardened to the cold to some degree, he used lots of seal oil to provide protection, so the cold rarely did any damage to his skin. He also had a thick beard—a beard that was already beginning to show signs of turning white which was another reminder to Nicholas of the passing of the seasons, and with them, the time left for handing on what he knew to a new generation.

"Ho!" Nicholas said, once the sleigh was clear of the stable, and suddenly all motion ceased.

"Now you all wait on a moment. There's more to do yet," he said.

The reindeer waited impatiently for the next instruction, but it was a while in coming. Nicholas was busy lighting the torches, rubbing more seal oil on his face, and closing the stable doors, least any wild animals should wander in looking for a place of warmth and comfort to shelter from the icy world.

Now all was ready. Nicholas climbed aboard.

"Ya," he said once more, and they were away at a quick pace, oil lights aglow, bells gently jingling, and torches flaming in the darkness, heading south at first, into the dark forest, following one of the ancient trails that meandered through its depths.

Nicholas knew all these roads exceedingly well, so he was not concerned about travelling them in the dark. The reindeer were also familiar with the tracks, and he and they knew every twist and turn, and exactly what lay around each bend. Such is the familiarity that comes of driving to and fro over many seasons.

Eventually the trail curved left towards the east. Heading now in an easterly direction, full of anticipation for the feasting and celebration that lay ahead, Nicholas relaxed a little allowing himself to enjoy the beauty of the winter's night—the vastness of the cloudless sky, the tiny stars twinkling in the heavens, the crisp virgin white landscape, the cold freshness of the air.

All proceeded as Nicholas had expected. He was heading to the place, a clearing in the forest by the side of the road, where he had prepared his Yule Log. He intended to wrap it with ropes, attach it to the rear of the sleigh and haul it back to his home. Then he would have to drag, lever, and roll it into his cabin and on to the fire. There it would burn brightly, adding light and warmth to his humble abode, and he knew that he would be well pleased with it once the task was done.

The sound of wolves in the forest accompanied Nicholas' journey. He had occasional glimpses of the creatures, racing along among the trees on his left flank, a close distance from the road, their eyes sometimes illuminated by the burning torches—eyrie points of light amidst the gloom of the dense wood. In the far distance he heard the baying of other packs. All seemed agitated that night, as if disturbed and frustrated by some phantom prey that eluded their keen sight and smell.

It is rare for a pack of wolves to be scarred. Whatever it was that had spooked them, must therefore have been be pretty frightening and powerful, for the wolves kept closer to Nicholas than they would normally, seeming to overcome their dislike of fire, in preference to whatever it was that was bothering them that night. They did not however venture too close to the sleigh to make Nicholas feel uncomfortable, but kept a distance, seemingly waiting for Nicholas to make a mistake, ever ready to pounce upon him and his reindeer should the opportunity arise.

This was one of the perils of travelling through the forest, but it was a risk that Nicholas had taken many times before.

"Why are they behaving like that?" Nicholas asked himself.

Although he was a little concerned about what might be causing the wolves to behave so strangely, he was not over worried. He maintained a watch on what was happening, keeping alert for any sudden changes in their behaviour.

Journeying onwards Nicholas saw familiar landmarks in the shapes and position of trees and large boulders by the side of the road, and in man-made items that had been placed at prominent positions by woodsmen, long ago, to guide travellers at night.

Other than the wolves, there was nothing at first that was markedly out of the ordinary, certainly nothing that would explain the strange sense that that was a special night. After travelling for half-an-hour, Nicholas noticed a yellow light ahead of him in the distance, faintly glowing in the darkness.

"That's peculiar," he thought to himself. "What can that be? Looks like a campfire, but who would be camping out on a night such as this?"

As he drew closer, his first assumption that it was a campfire was confirmed—the flickering of the light meant that it could only be such. But the mystery of why there should be a fire burning in the depths of the forest on such an extremely cold winter's night, remained just that—a mystery.

"Looks as if someone may be in trouble," Nicholas said to the reindeer.

Eventually Nicholas' expectations of finding someone camping were realised. There ahead of him by the side of the road he saw the fire that was the source of the flickering yellow light. Seated next to it was someone trying to keep warm, wrapped in blankets, hands held out in a vain attempt to feel the warmth of the meagre blaze.

"Now, what on earth is going on here?" Nicholas quietly asked himself.

Nicholas pulled up, halting the sleigh just as it drew adjacent to the flames. He could see now that there was an old man sitting there, a very old man, which somewhat surprised Nicholas, for elderly people tended not to venture out during the cold season, it being much harder for them to cope with the freezing conditions.

On stopping, Nicholas paused for a moment, unsure of himself. He was being cautious. He looked around wondering if this was a trap for he did not assume that all people he met were innocent and harmless. The forest was a lonely place, and it was not unheard of for bandits to waylay travellers and woodsmen, robbing them of their possessions, and sometimes killing them. This happened occasionally, but only in the warmer times of the year. Most robbers were interested in easy pickings and were not inclined to venture out in inclement weather, so on a mid-winter's night, with temperatures well below freezing, the chance that it was someone with evil intent was small, yet it was wise to be careful.

So Nicholas looked behind him, glanced over to his right, studied the road ahead, and then once more looked to his left where the old man sat. The fellow did not look up, seemingly lost in his own little world by the small fire that appeared on the point of faltering, of being extinguished.

It was a rather sad and pathetic scene that Nicholas observed. There before him, an elderly man, probably cast out by his relatives, left to fend for himself in the cold.

The man had no possessions by his side. All he had to protect him from the weather and to keep himself warm was what he was wearing and a few blankets. He looked as though he had been abandoned by the roadside, just left there, on his own, to await his fate. Nicholas began to feel pity for the stranger.

"Who would do such a thing?" Nicholas asked himself. "How cruel."

Nicholas knew instinctively that he had to help. He was a compassionate person and he could not leave the stranger to suffer and to die. So his mind was made up. He would take the old man with him, give him shelter for a few days, and when the Yuletide celebrations were over, he would take him to the nearest settlement and see if anyone could help find the stranger's relatives.

There are occasions however, when things are not what they seem. Details present themselves to the senses that point to one conclusion, then, on closer exploration, one finds that the initial assumption is wrong. Nicholas was about to discover for himself that this could be so.

CHAPTER TWO

THE EARTH SPIRIT

Nicholas stepped out of the sleigh and began to move towards the fire. The old man did not look up nor did he register that he was aware of Nicholas' arrival. Closer and closer Nicholas moved, but still no reaction from the stranger sitting by the fire. All through his approach, Nicholas was ignored. It was though Nicholas did not exist, as if he were an unseen phantom, a white spirit, concealed from view against the backdrop of the snow-covered landscape.

On realising he had not been noticed Nicholas spoke, raising his voice least the stranger were hard of hearing.

"Hello there," Nicholas said with a friendly tone. There was no response. Nicholas kept on moving forward. "Hello there," he repeated. Still no response. Nicholas reached the fire. He crouched down so that his eyes were level with the old man, who had now, at last, begun to respond to Nicholas' presence.

"What are you doing, camping out on a night such as this?"

Nicholas asked in a kindly way.

The old man had been slowly lifting his head, and now he was staring straight into Nicholas' eyes. Nicholas was startled, for the look on the stranger's face was disturbing and unearthly, and his gaze penetrating and unsettling. The old man's eyes were like nothing Nicholas had seen before, for in the darkness, lit only by the light from the fire, they appeared to be just black circles surrounded by the whites of the eyeballs. In the blackness of the old man's eyes Nicholas saw the flames reflected, and it was as though the fire burned within the stranger. Looking into these shadowy spots was similar to peering into deep pools of icy water, where, hidden below the surface, there was a world unseen and unknown and potentially very dangerous.

The old man spoke, saying, "What do you want? Who disturbs me on this night of all nights?"

The tone of his voice conveyed displeasure with Nicholas. The stranger seemed to be out of humour with himself and disinclined to engage in conversation.

"My name is Nicholas, and I stopped because I thought that you might be in need of help."

"I don't need help," returned the old man, with more than a hint of contempt in his voice.

"It's a custom in these parts to help others," Nicholas began to explain. "I couldn't just pass by and ignore you."

"Custom! I do not wish to know about your inclination to help others, and care even less."

The old man had responded with a tone that Nicholas found offensive.

"Then you must be a newcomer to these parts, for I must say that I have never seen you before," Nicholas said.

"I am no newcomer," the old man firmly stated.

"Then who are you, if you don't mind me asking?"

"Mind! Well I would have minded in time gone by, but it doesn't matter now. It's all over for me," the stranger said, enigmatically.

"What do you mean? What's all over for you?"

"You ask a question, then before I have given you an answer, you interrupt me and ask another," the old man said, with a smirk on his face.

From this observant response, Nicholas quickly realised that the elderly stranger had a sharp mind. His exterior conveyed an impression of a great age, greater than Nicholas had ever seen, which was unusual, but mentally the man was alert and agile.

"I'm sorry," Nicholas returned, "please do continue."

"You ask who I am. It's not a question that I would normally answer. I do not spend my time telling mere mortal folk such as you, who and what I am. Alas tonight is different. I have been drawn here, nay, I have chosen to come here, because of events that I did not want to happen. The thing that I have resisted for as long as the world has existed, is, it seems, about to happen. I came here to be present and to do what I can to prevent it. Then it starts—you come along, you that, I have no doubt, will take some part in the events of this night."

The stranger stopped for a brief moment, and then resumed.

"Enough! I have said more than I intended, but I will tell you who I am, for tonight I am feeling kindly towards you so I will make an exception. Perhaps in explaining to you about myself I can change the course of events."

There was a sly look on the stranger's face that Nicholas did not notice. Nicholas was the type of person that spoke honestly and plainly to people, and had little of experience of those that sought to manipulate circumstances to their advantage, saying one thing when their true feelings were inclined to entirely different thoughts. So Nicholas did not recognise that this was what the old man was doing.

What the stranger had said so far sounded peculiar to Nicholas. He was mystified by the old man's words and he was interested to know more. So Nicholas expectantly listened while the old man went about implementing his plan to achieve an outcome that was to his liking.

"I am," the old man began, "the one who has watched over this world for so long, since humans took their first faltering steps! I am the seasons, the wind, the rain, the ice, and the snow. Nature's harvest—the fruits that you collect, the trees that you fell, and the animals that you hunt—all these come from me. I give you everything that you have. I am the one by which you live. I am the one that brings order to your lives. I am…" Here he paused for effect, then continued, "I am the Spirit of the Earth. I am the Earth Spirit."

The old man had become animated. His voice conveyed passion, and Nicholas had the impression that the stranger believed in what he was saying. But to Nicholas the spoken words only suggested madness. Perhaps the stranger was not so mentally capable after all?

The stranger continued to speak, saying, "I see from the look on your face that you do not believe me. Let me ask you a question. You have heard of the Spirit of the Earth, the one you and your people call the Earth Spirit?"

Nicholas did of course know of the Earth Spirit, it being part of the culture of his people. So he responded appropriately.

"Yes of course," replied Nicholas, unsure of where this was leading.

"Good I am pleased to hear it. It would not do, not to know about the Earth Spirit."

"And your point is?" Nicholas asked.

"My point, as you put it, is that I am the Earth Spirit! I am the one who you and your people celebrate and honour. Here in this place, here in the bleak mid-winter, at Yuletide, I choose to reveal myself to you. I, the one your people have respected for so long, for a countless age! I, master of this world in which you live."

Nicholas was taken aback by this, for he did not in all truth expect an old man sitting by a dying fire in the middle of the forest on a cold winter's night to claim to be the Earth Spirit. Not that he gave credence to such a thing, for he knew that it was nothing more than a tale—a mystical component of his peoples' folklore. No doubt it served to help explain the puzzle that was nature, but it was to Nicholas just an invention that fulfilled a human need to believe in powerful forces shaping the destiny of humankind. Only the simplest of minds would take the belief literally.

However the old man had not finished speaking, having just paused for a few moments to allow the meaning of his great revelation to have an impact. He looked long and hard at Nicholas and then asked, "Am I to be pushed aside in favour of Him? Are you going to let that happen?"

As the stranger said this, his tone had changed to one of anger, and he gestured, pointing further up the road towards the east, where Nicholas to his surprise, could make out yet another light glowing in the distance.

On seeing this it occurred to Nicholas that the old man might be part of a larger group of people, and for some reason not clear to Nicholas, the stranger had chosen to camp separately from them. Perhaps the old man had fallen out with his fellow travellers, for a traveller is what he now assumed the stranger was. However, another possibility presented itself to Nicholas, a new thought, providing an explanation better suited to the circumstances. This was, as Nicholas had begun to discover for himself, that the fellow was of such an unsociable disposition and so mentally deranged, that his presence with the others was not welcome, and perhaps there was an agreement that the man would camp on his own.

Nicholas was in no doubt that the stranger also preferred to be on his own. Age had clearly wearied this fellow, and turned him into an ill-natured person, for this Nicholas supposed, was what had happened to the slightly crazy old man who sat in front of him. Time can do that to people, but not to all, for there are those who grow old yet still retain the optimism of youth and the ability to recognise the good in folk.

For the old man, so it appeared, age had been less kind. With the passing of the years the fellow had become grumpy and sour—characteristics that the stranger displayed in abundance. This is the conclusion that Nicholas had reached based on the words spoken, the manner of their delivery, and the attitude displayed. Nicholas was about to discover however that there was more to the old man than was at first apparent and that he was indeed exactly who he said he was—the Earth Spirit!

Although Nicholas was ready to believe that the old man's unsociable demeanour and his mental problems might be the reason that he was camped separately from the others, doubt began to creep in when Nicholas started to wonder why there was such a large distance between the two campsites. Surely they would be much closer together? This was indeed a strange circumstance and Nicholas was resolved to discover more.

Nicholas decided to humour the old man to try to find out who was camped along the road, so he said, "I don't understand what you are talking about." Then Nicholas asked, "Who has pushed you aside and who is camped in the distance?"

"These are things that you would not grasp," responded the old man, with a dismissive tone, looking once again into the dying flames of the fire.

Nicholas was not going to let matters rest, so he persisted with his questioning. "You said that my people respected you.

What did you mean by that?"

The stranger looked up, staring again directly into Nicholas' eyes, with his penetrating gaze, which made Nicholas feel uncomfortable.

"I can see that you are the persistent sort," the old man said, "but you're wasting your time with me. I'm all right here on my own. Now move on," adding by way of a finishing enigmatic remark, "and if you know what's good for you you'll turn back and head home now, while you can."

There was a tone in the voice that indicated that this last part of his statement was not advice, but an instruction.

Nicholas was unsure what to say and what to do. He stood up for a moment, since cramp was beginning to affect his legs from crouching down. He looked about him. There was no-one else to be seen, no-one who could perhaps explain—just the glow of the fire burning in the distance. The wolves Nicholas noticed, were watching the scene, but had increased their distance from him, seeming to be wary of the stranger, which only made Nicholas even more curious.

Nicholas found the old man disturbing and he was not keen to linger. Apart from the fellow's unsociable manner, he also had an aura that was disquieting, and his eyes were barely human, being more like those of a wild animal, and whatever difficulty the stranger might be in, he seemed determined to be left alone. But Nicholas, being a kind person, was reluctant to leave the old man, for it did not seem right to do so. Crouching down once more, Nicholas persisted with his questioning.

"I know that you want to be left to yourself, but pray tell me what you are talking about. I can't just ride off leaving you here on your own. Why do you say I should turn back?"

A cold dark look had appeared on the face of the stranger in response to this further probing.

"You are a persistent fool," the old man said angrily. "I see however that I am not going to be rid of you until your curiosity is satisfied, so I will tell you." He then added, now with menace, "Then you will leave me and do as I say and go home."

There was no mistaking the meaning and the tone. This was an instruction. It was one that Nicholas felt that he would have to follow in part, for while he had no intention of heading back home as yet, the sinister way in which the stranger had just spoken, had convinced Nicholas that the old man was better left well alone.

"All right," replied Nicholas. "Have it your way. Speak and then I will leave, but where I go next is my business, not yours."

This was the cue for the old man to begin, and he did, but Nicholas perceived that the stranger was not at all pleased with what Nicholas had just said.

But the old man's attitude suddenly changed. From being cold and unfriendly, seemingly resenting Nicholas' presence, the stranger warmed to his visitor. Nicholas was surprised by this, for, but a moment before, the old man had been threatening towards him. Now the stranger seemed most welcoming and anxious for Nicholas to hear what he had to say. What he said, however, Nicholas was not prepared for.

"You're young," observed the stranger. "I am old. Very old! I am old as time. I have been around for as long as your people have existed, and longer. I am the ways that your people have followed for countless seasons. Every mid-winter, even though many of you have now forgotten, all your Yuletide celebrations, festivities and your rituals were originally designed to do honour to me. I am the foundation of your life."

The old man halted for a moment, pausing to take breath. His eyes had been ablaze with passion as he had spoken these words, and now he was coldly staring at Nicholas. However, refreshed with air, he resumed.

"Look into the fire my visitor," the old man demanded.

"What!" Nicholas said with surprised look on his face.

"Just look! Don't speak. Look into the flames," the stranger responded, showing impatience.

The old man's mood had swung again, so Nicholas did as he was instructed, and saw only the weak flames of a dying fire. Then suddenly the flames began to grow stronger as if willed on to do so by the old man. They grew taller and gave off more heat, and soon, there before Nicholas was a blazing fire worthy of any seasoned woodsman.

The flames danced before Nicholas, fanned by the wind, which had unexpectedly arisen from nothing in a matter of seconds, stirring up loose snow as it did so, sending the white powder into Nicholas' face. Gazing into the fire, and occasionally brushing the snow from his face, Nicholas began to make out shapes in the flickering dancing flames. Indistinct at first, gradually they took on human form, until before Nicholas, living within the fire were scenes being played out, as if he were watching them on a stage far away, small but still clear to see.

"Do you see them?" the old man demanded to know.

"Yes I see what seem to be people," replied Nicholas, unsure of himself.

"Good. Now watch and learn."

So this is what Nicholas did and what he witnessed he did not care for at all. In the flickering orange flames he saw men going about their daily business—cutting timber, harvesting crops, eating, sleeping, living, and dying. Now, it was not all the images that Nicholas found disturbing, for in themselves many seemed innocuous. However, interspersed with these he saw events and actions that did not sit well with his own way of living and his notions of what was right and proper.

In one incident Nicholas saw a young boy, hungry, begging for food, but no-one would give him any at all. In another there was an old man, worn down by life, unable to look after himself, but with his usefulness gone, he was just left to die, with not a soul bothering to take care of him. Then Nicholas saw greedy people accumulating great wealth at the expense of those around them, who were for the most part poor and weak. He also saw images of violence where men took other peoples' possessions and made them their own. There were also pictures of war, terrible conflicts, in which it seemed that countless numbers of people died. Frighteningly, Nicholas also saw narrow-minded men, influenced by evil masquerading as good, who, being full of hatred and bitterness, were prepared to inflict death and suffering on the innocent to further their misguided beliefs.

Nicholas watched with growing disgust, until he could look no more and he turned his head away slightly to his left, looking down at the snow, feeling sick at the sights that the fire had revealed. As Nicholas did so the dancing flames died down and the wind suddenly dropped and disappeared as mysteriously and unexpectedly as it had first appeared. Nicholas looked up slightly surprised, but also relieved for he did not want to witness any more of the visions that the fire had to reveal.

"What is this you are showing me? These are terrible spectacles," Nicholas said.

The old man sniggered. "These are the pictures of life as it was, is and will be in the future. What you have just seen, is nature's way! Humans are just like other animals, young stranger—they are born, they live and they die, and that is it. If you are not strong and take what you need, take what you want, then those that are stronger than you are, those that are more determined, they will take from you. Look at the world. Is that not how animals exist?"

The old man did not wait for Nicholas to answer, but continued. "I say look after yourself first. I say when someone hurts or harms you, then you do the same back. I say this world is yours for the taking so take it and use it as you think fit, for yourself. Think of yourself first. Other peoples' problems are not yours. The weak have no place in the world. Leave them to their fate. You live once, and once only, so make the most of it. The world is a cruel hard place and the only way to survive is to be cruel and hard yourself. Life will grind you down if you let it, so grind it down first. Don't let anyone get the better of you.

Don't trust, don't share, and don't bother. Just look after the most important person in the world—yourself!"

Nicholas listened with growing horror to this tirade of bitterness and selfishness. In it he recognised some truth. Yes, this was how some people lived their lives, in varying degrees, but not everyone was that heartless and selfish. To Nicholas the old man's message was one of hopelessness and despair, and it did not find any resonance with Nicholas.

Instinctively Nicholas rose and backed away from the stranger. "This is not how we live" Nicholas said. "This is a recipe for a world of destruction and hatred."

"Come back here and listen to me," demanded the old man. "I did not invite you here. You came of your own free will. You insisted on talking to me. You are the one who asked questions. Now listen!"

The stranger had become angry and agitated, but as suddenly as this black mood had descended upon him, it was gone. When old man spoke again he was calmer.

"Ah! See! You're infected already," the old man said with less emotion, as if resigned to some inevitability that Nicholas was unaware of.

Continuing the stranger said, "What you witnessed in the flames, is nature's way. Animals of all kinds live by these laws.

Is it not so that once an animal becomes old and weak, it just crawls away and dies? Do you see wolves caring for the weak among them? No, young man, you don't! Never! This is how it should be for humankind. This is what I represent. This is my way, the ways of the Earth Spirit, and it is necessary. Part of the order of things, but it seems that my time in this world is nearly over, and it's precisely because of people such as you, who think you know better than I. You with your compassion and notions of helping others. Go on, be gone with you! Leave me alone. No doubt you want to go and see Him, for I can tell that you are one of His sort, but I warn you, you had better make haste and head back home now, for unless you do, you will rue the night that you met Him."

Nicholas wanted to know to whom the old man was referring. He wondered for a moment if he dared to ask any further questions, fearing that to do so might annoy the stranger even more and push him deeper into gloom, even provoke the old man to violence. Nicholas, however, did not want to leave without first asking about this other person. So he plucked up the courage to ask.

"Who is it that you are talking about? Who is this other person? Who is this *Him* that you refer to?"

"My nemesis," replied the stranger without hesitation. "It is

He who has worked against me all my existence. At the beginning His power was weak. I was the powerful one. It is I that have dominated the world, making sure that its natural order is maintained. Those that are strongest do best, those that aren't ... That's nature! Alas His strength grows. Slowly over time, as I have kept watch over the world, His influence has become evident, and now He challenges me. This is my world, and it is doomed. This I sense. He will win in the end. This I now know, but I will not go down without a fight. Mark my words young man. I have reserves of strength left, and as long as that is so, I will resist. You will see. My time draws to a close, but it is not yet ended."

Once more the old man had become agitated and angry and Nicholas judged that it was best not to make more enquiries least the stranger became aggressive. Nicholas stood up once more. Looking down on the stranger Nicholas' primary feeling was one of pity; pity for a man who seemed to be beyond hope, a man whose feeling were entombed in ice that no amount of compassion could break or melt.

Nicholas did not know what to make of this stranger with his crazy words. In other circumstances Nicholas would have concluded that the old man was indeed mad. Nothing else, under more normal conditions, could account for the bizarre words that the stranger had spoken. If matters had been that straightforward,

Nicholas could understand why the old man's companions, if he had any, would not have wanted him to camp with them—the further away that the old man was, the better! Yes, this would have explained everything if it had not been for the terrible visions in the fire! All would be clear if it were not for those heartless images, and the old man's strange dark eyes, and the atmosphere that the stranger generated, a sensation that he, Nicholas, and the wolves with their more receptive and keener senses, all found disturbing.

It was time for Nicholas to leave. No good could come of lingering longer. There were many unanswered questions running through Nicholas' mind, but no answers to be found there. Perhaps at the next campsite, along the road he was travelling that night, he would find better explanations for what had transpired with the old man.

So Nicholas tried to find some soothing and kind words on which to depart, not wanting to leave abruptly or to cause offence.

"I will go now," Nicholas began, "but I ask one more time, will you not come with me? I can take you to the fire that burns so brightly in the distance."

"That fire that you see burning has nothing to do with me. That is His doing not mine," the old man emphatically stated. "I travel this world alone. So go to Him, for I see that you are beyond hope. But if you have any sense, you'll head home now while you can."

As he uttered these closing words the old man glanced towards the east, where the other light that Nicholas had seen was still glowing strong and bright amidst the darkness of the night.

The stranger held his gaze for a few seconds. The expression on his face spoke the words that the now silent old man did not utter with his voice, and then the fellow returned to staring into the dying flames of his fire. The stranger said no more—no single utterance, no final words to send Nicholas on his way. There were no wishes for a safe journey. No messages to carry.

The old man's stone-faced silence was a signal to Nicholas to depart, and to tell the truth, Nicholas did not want to stay. Nicholas could see that the old man was full of hatred for life. The fellow was, for Nicholas, as mysterious to him as he had been on his first stopping and stepping forth to greet the old man. The words that the stranger had spoken were not those of a normal individual, and this had only added to the mystery.

"Very well," Nicholas finally said, trying to remain polite, for in truth he was more than a little weary with the old man's rather rude attitude towards him, as well as the stranger's disturbing talk. "I will leave, but I'll be coming back this way later, so if you change your mind, I'm willing to help."

The old man did not respond to this, and just waved Nicholas away while looking into the flames of the dying fire.

Nicholas turned and walked back to his sleigh. When seated he glanced once more at the stranger, and then set off, heading towards the light in the distance in the hope of finding an explanation for the old man and his odd behaviour.

The distant light beckoned as if calling to Nicholas and with hope for a better and warmer welcome, Nicholas resumed his journey, the sleigh sliding over the frozen snow, oil lights aglow, bells gently jingling, and torches flaming in the darkness.

He had not gone far, but a few short steps for the reindeer, when a most peculiar event happened. Instinctively, out of a natural concern for the stranger, Nicholas glanced back over his shoulder. Nicholas wanted to check to see if the old man had seen the folly of his attitude, and if he was signalling to Nicholas to come back. What Nicholas saw, or more correctly what he did not see, shocked him!

Nicholas pulled up suddenly, halting the sleigh, rose and gazed into the darkness. Where was the fire? It was gone, along with the old man. The sleigh had only moved a short distance down the track. It had been but a matter of seconds since Nicholas had glanced at the stranger, but now there was no sign of old man and his encampment. The mysterious character had vanished without trace. The old man had gone, disappeared as though he had never been, leaving no obvious signs that he had ever been there at all.

Nicholas leapt from the sleigh, and grabbing one of the flaming torches, he ran back the short distance to where the fire had been burning. There was nothing to be seen except the footprints in the snow that Nicholas had left, but of the old man and his campfire there was no indication that they had ever been there. The snow lay undisturbed, virgin white, crisp, and clean. Not a trace of the stranger could be found!

Nicholas glanced around. Yes, no doubt about it, this was the right spot.

"Am I seeing things?" Nicholas asked himself aloud. There was no-one to answer this question, just the emptiness of the wilderness, devoid of his fellow creatures. No-one present who could shed some light on what was indeed a strange circumstance, or provide explanations for a mystery that seemed to be growing by the minute.

Now, it was not unheard of for people spending time out in the forest to imagine things. The wild places of the world can do that to men. Nicholas had heard stories of foresters who had claimed to have seen peculiar creatures in the dark woods, but these were just tales. Nicholas however had never experienced anything like this, nor had any of his friends. This was the type of story that was repeated in the warmth and security of the home, usually over a warming drink, on cold dark nights, while sitting by a blazing fire. Stories told in safe places, where no harm could befall the tellers and the listeners, tempted the imagination to ponder the notion that there were mysteries to life, things that could not be explained. But these were not thoughts that one entertained beyond the warmth and security of the fireside, and certainly not ones to contemplate out in the harshness of the forest on a night such as that, when even the most experienced were at risk if they did not keep their wits about them.

A growling sound filtered into Nicholas' consciousness. It was the wolves! Sensing an opportunity and with the fear of the old man now gone, a fear which had previously held them back, the pack were drawing closer, mouths drooling, eyes green and hungry and firmly set on their prey—Nicholas!

Suddenly alert to the approaching danger, Nicholas reacted instinctively. This was not the first time that he had been confronted by a pack of hungry wolves. On the last occasion Nicholas had faced five of the creatures and had driven them off with a combination of a large bladed knife, courage, and a little bit of good fortune, for they had been a rather timid bunch as it turned out, as wolves went, and must have had little stomach for a fight. This time it was different. There were more of them, perhaps ten or more, and they were hungry. Very hungry! The hard winter had taken its toll on them, and their desire to fill their bellies had diminished their fear of men with fire. The pack leader was also bold and fearless.

Between Nicholas and the sleigh there was a distance of no more than 100 metres. Was there enough time to make the dash back to the sanctuary that the sleigh offered? The gap between Nicholas and the wolves was closing. They were fast movers and could easily outrun a man. Nicholas judged that he was too far away from the sleigh. As soon as he turned to run the wolves would sense victory and would be upon him in a matter of seconds. Nicholas knew that there was no way he could escape. For all Nicholas' experience, he had allowed his curiosity to place himself in a position of danger.

Keeping the wolves in sight Nicholas started to walk backwards, very slowly, retracing his steps, holding the flaming torch towards the horde, waving it around to make it appear more threatening. Nicholas knew however that backing away in this manner would only encourage the wolves to become bolder. Retreat in the face of such a large number of desperate creatures was a sure signal to them that they were in control. Yet to stand firm in face of such a determined pack was no option either. Poor

Nicholas was faced with a terrible dilemma.

Nicholas knew all this, but had judged that the best course of action was to retreat, for that at least would move him closer to the sleigh. This was a place of relative safety, if its flaming torches were enough to discourage the animals, which Nicholas did have some doubts about.

Nicholas drew his long bladed knife, sharp and dangerous, and prepared for battle. Closer they came, and closer to the sleigh moved Nicholas.

In the end it was a finely balanced thing. For a moment Nicholas' fate hovered between life and death, but life prevailed. What saved him in the end was a moment's hesitation by the lead wolf. Holding back for too long, the pack had allowed Nicholas time to draw closer to the sleigh. Too close, for the fear of the flames issuing from the torches eventually began to overcome their hunger. Nicholas could see this and turned, ran and then leaped into the sleigh. He was safe for the moment, but there was no time to lose. Replacing the torch in its holder he shouted at the reindeer and once more he was on his way along the track towards the light that still burned in the distance.

The wolves for their part on losing their meal, at least for the moment, skulked back into the forest, occasionally stopping to howl as if in frustration, and they began once more to follow

Nicholas, keeping their distance, but ever ready to strike should the opportunity for a meal present itself again.

Nicholas was relieved and made a mental note not to take such a foolish action again. Ahead, the light grew brighter as Nicholas approached, and he wondered if this too would turn out to be an illusion, for an illusion is what Nicholas had concluded was probably what he had seen—not an old man sitting by a meagre fire, but a trick of his own imagination, and one that had nearly cost Nicholas his life. This he believed was a likely explanation for the strange event, for the visions in the fire. Nicholas also considered it possible that the old man might have been a ghost, a spectra, not of this world, but of another that Nicholas knew nothing of and did not want to contemplate. Perhaps the old man was indeed the Earth Spirit, but this did not matter to Nicholas, for he did not want to meet the fellow again. An invention of his an imagination! A ghost! The Earth Spirit! At that time and place it was of no interest to Nicholas which. This he would ponder at some later moment, when he was safely back in his warm and cosy home. For the time being Nicholas was focused on ensuring that he was safe from the wolves.

So it was that Nicholas' first encounter that night, with a spectre calling itself the Earth Spirit, came to an end, and his next meeting, with another and very different character, began.

CHAPTER THREE

THE WHITE ANGEL

Onward Nicholas travelled as he raced away from the danger that had nearly been the end of him. But the wolves did not give up and leave, but followed behind. Eventually catching him up, keeping once more to his left flank, as they had done before, they remained within the dense wood that lined Nicholas' route.

Plunging forward in their endless pursuit, they darted among the trees, showing their agility by rapidly dashing left and right to avoid colliding with the trunks. They were a determined pack, that is for sure, but they would that night meet their match. Not yet though, for this still lay ahead.

With every second that passed, with every moment of time, Nicholas drew closer to the distant light. As he did so it grew larger, its luminosity increasing with each step forward that the galloping reindeer did take.

On approaching the source of this illumination, a welcome sight began to reveal itself to Nicholas' eyes in the form of a blazing fire, casting orange and yellow light upon the trees, chasing away the darkness.

This was indeed a fire to behold! It was no meagre affair. Although not large, its intensity was evident in the flames that leapt from it and its radiance seemed to be growing. Standing in sharp contrast to the old man's fire, which, with the passing of each minute had become dimmer, fading away, hovering on the verge of vanishing from the world as though it had never been, this new light shone out like a beacon, illuminating a dark world, offering a guide for all lost travellers on the road of life.

On drawing up adjacent to the blaze, Nicholas looked about him. Sat by the fire was another stranger, this time a young man dressed in white. To Nicholas' surprise the stranger was not wearing warm winter clothes, but was attired in light thin garments that could serve no purpose to protect the man from the wintry environment that surrounded him.

Nevertheless the young man seemed not at all to be affected by the cold. His countenance was far more welcoming than that of the previous character Nicholas had encountered upon that strange night. This came as a relief to Nicholas who was sorely tired of the old man's shifting moods and aggression. As for the wolves, there was now no sign of them. They, it appeared, did not care for the sight upon which Nicholas' eyes looked and had retreated into the blackness of the forest, hiding, but still no doubt waiting as before, for a chance to attack.

The sight that presented itself to Nicholas' gaze was indeed agreeable, for the fire not only emitted a great light, but also much heat, which Nicholas could feel even from the sleigh, and the young stranger, with his angelic features, seemed to add to the warmth. Yet there was an aspect to the picture before him that was not as earthly as it should have been. It had a quality about it, an atmosphere, which spoke of other realms, of other worlds, far beyond the reach of mortal creatures.

Nicholas left the sleigh and walked towards the young man. As he did so Nicholas' large brown snow boots crunched on the white snow with each step that he took. Moving the short distance between the sleigh and fire did not take long, but in those few brief moments Nicholas wondered if this stranger too was an illusion, or perhaps just a ghost of the night, though he certainly seemed real!

The young man rose as Nicholas approached, saying as he did so, "Ah! A visitor! You are most welcome on this cold night. Please come and sit by my fire and warm yourself."

Nicholas detected immediately that he was in the company of a more sociable person, someone who would be better company than the old man had been.

As soon as Nicholas stood in the young stranger's presence Nicholas sensed it! Standing close now, Nicholas' initial feelings were confirmed—the youthful person who had so warmly greeted him did indeed have an unusual, but calming aura. Nicholas had never experienced such a sensation before, and he liked it very much, seeming to remind him of feelings long lost to his memory.

Now it is sometimes so that those who are old—as demonstrated by the old man, the one who had called himself the Earth Spirit—present a cruel and hard image to their fellow creatures. Age for such people follows a destructive course, wearing them down, sapping their will to live, reducing their compassion and humanity, and turning those that tread this unfortunate path into heartless people. To be free then from the cynicism that age so often brings! To be fresh! To find novelty in life! To be surprised! To discover new things in familiar scenes! To still be enchanted by the world with all its strangeness, wonders, and mysteries! This surely is the value of youth!

Age however does not invariably bring pessimism and despair. It does not have to be like this. There is no natural law which decrees that the passing years have to weary, or transform to stone, or create bitterness and indifference. This surely is a matter of individual choice and disposition, and is a course of events that can, upon conscious decision, be avoided.

Time does to people, as people do to themselves. To grow old, yet still to retain the optimism of youth and a positive view of humanity, this surely is the path all should seek to follow. Not to allow age to dim the ability to distinguish between the minority who behave badly, and the majority who struggle through life trying to live a good existence, this must be the right perspective. For as surely as all are tempted and challenged by the many distractions that can lead even the most determined to go astray, for those that do succumb, there are far more that do not.

For reasons that Nicholas did not perceive, these positive thoughts and feelings presented themselves to Nicholas now that he was close to the stranger, as though they were flowing out from the young man. Optimism seemed to fill the air. Goodness and joy radiated from the young stranger, making Nicholas experience warmth and happiness. This was the influence that the stranger was having upon Nicholas. For just as the old man, the Earth Spirit, had shown to Nicholas all that was negative about human existence, this young fellow, even without speaking, was doing exactly the opposite.

Aware that the old man had probably been no more than a phantom of the night, perhaps even a trick of Nicholas' mind, the question that jumped into Nicholas' consciousness found quick and sudden articulation.

Standing before the blazing fire, and not waiting for the stranger to speak again, Nicholas blurted out the question so prominent in his thoughts, "Are you real? Or are you just an apparition?" he asked.

The young man smiled, but did not answer. Motioning to Nicholas to take a seat upon a barrel covered with fur that was placed opposite to where the young man had been seated but a moment before, they both sat down. Gazing in silence at each other, Nicholas had the distinct impression that the stranger had been expecting him.

Real did the barrel feel to Nicholas, as did the heat from the fire, which created a warming sensation, one that was most pleasant amidst the snow and ice. But Nicholas recalled that he had felt the meagre heat given off by the old man's fire and in the end the elderly stranger had turned out to be a spectre of that Yuletide Eve. Nicholas, aware of this, was expecting the young man to turn out just the same.

Nicholas had started to wonder what these peculiar encounters were all about and why this was happening to him. As he did so he looked at his host, noticing that the young man's eyes had nothing of the darkness of the old man's. There was light and hope in these eyes, rather than coldness and despair.

The silence Nicholas found uncomfortable. He had so many

questions to ask, and was on the verge of repeating his previous question, when the young man began to speak.

"I suppose that you are wondering about the old man that you encountered further up the road?" the young stranger asked. "The one who called himself the Earth Spirit? The one who disappeared as soon as you had left him?"

That the young stranger knew of Nicholas' encounter with the Earth Spirit, and that the old man had vanished on Nicholas' departure, only confirmed Nicholas' suspicions that the two strangers were in some way connected, and that perhaps therefore, this young man might be able to explain the events that had just transpired.

"So you know about him?" Nicholas enquired in a tone that conveyed no surprise.

"Yes indeed I do," replied the young man.

"And his sudden disappearance? That too it seems you know about?" Nicholas asked, seeking confirmation.

"Yes, I do," the stranger confirmed.

"That is why I asked if you are real," Nicholas stated, "for it seems that tonight I am seeing people that do not exist and who can vanish at a whim."

"Let me assure you that it's not your imagination that is creating what you are seeing. He, like I, does exist, but not in your world. We dwell elsewhere, in a place where no human form can pass. But this point is not of importance at this moment. Be calm my friend. I can do you no harm for it is not my way to injure any creature. I appear before you for a reason, but first let me explain to you about the old man that you so recently met."

Nicholas was all attention. He felt no disquiet or alarm, nor was he disturbed by the young stranger's admission that he was not of the physical world.

"There are two sides to human life," continued the young man. "Darkness and light are to be found in all people. What you should know, is that the Earth Spirit represents the darker side of humanity. He is everything that is miserable and brutal about folk. He holds back humans, maintaining them in a primitive state no better than animals. His way denies the spark of life, the light that is within all. There is nothing but harshness, pain, and suffering in his way. All he offers is life lived by the ways of nature with no prospect of rising above the material world and seeing the universe for what it is."

The young man paused for a moment to check that Nicholas was following.

"Do you understand what I am saying?" he asked of Nicholas.

"Yes. I think I do. What you say corresponds with the impression that I gained of the old man."

"But what is important are the consequences," the young man stated. "This is what you should realise."

"Consequences?" Nicholas asked, slightly puzzled.

"Yes consequences. Let me explain. If his ways are adhered to, then there can be no future for humankind. You will all sink into a deep abyss of eternal darkness. The Earth Spirit represents not just the dark side of human life, but also the worst human characteristics. A more a miserable, spiteful, and destructive spirit you could not find. His way can only lead to the destruction of humanity. Now I know that might be hard to understand, to visualise, but believe me, it does!"

Nicholas did not know how to respond to what the young stranger had just said and was lost for words, for such notions were not ones that he had contemplated before. However, the young man had more to say so there was no need at that moment for Nicholas to say anything.

"The old man," the young stranger continued, "he is of the past. He is representative of the world as it has been. His are the ways of the selfish, the brutal, the unforgiving. No love, compassion or forgiveness will you find within him."

The young stranger painted a gloomy picture with his words, which made Nicholas feel a little depressed, but then the young man began to speak in more optimistic tones, and Nicholas' cheer returned, reminding him of the good mood on which the night had begun. It was, after all, the evening of the main Yuletide celebration and not a time for dark and depressive thoughts.

"Enough of the Earth Spirit, though," the young man finally said. "It is not my purpose to detail his perspective on the world, and how he would have you conduct your lives. That his way binds you in the darkness through living by harsh, inflexible, and dogmatic rules, this I think is self evident from what you have seen of him already. Now to explain my presence, for I have no doubt that you are also wondering why I am camped here on such a cold night?"

"Yes indeed," replied Nicholas, who had now found a response to what was being said to him. "This is a most peculiar circumstance. I have lived all my life in the forest, and never have I encountered people outdoors on a cold winter's night with little in the way of adequate shelter and clothing. Then I find that I have not an old man met, but a spirit. That you know of this, that you also admit to being a spirit, that you show no concern for the effects of the cold weather, and that the wolves do not worry you, speaks to me of strangeness beyond comprehension. Yet, having just met the Earth Spirit and experienced his ways first hand, I have to say that I sense far more of joy about you than of woe."

"That is correct my friend," the young man said softly in response to this. "Freezing conditions and hungry wolves will not harm me. No force of evil or of nature can hurt me. And as for joy, this is the very essence of my being here. It is what has brought me to your world. And tonight it is not only cold that I have encountered. I have travelled far and wide this evening, visiting many places, hot and cold, wet and dry, moderate and extreme. All sorts of weather have I experienced. I have seen both deserts of sand and of snow. Many different people have I met. I have stood before men, both rich and poor, young and old, well of health and those who are inflicted with terrible diseases, and this is my final appearance. You are the last person to whom I will speak on this most glorious of nights, and my purpose in doing all this, I hear you wondering, of visiting so many places in one night, is to deliver a message."

"A message! You are a messenger! Pray tell me more about this message," Nicholas said with some excitement, for the young man had created a sense of wondrous anticipation that had affected Nicholas.

"Yes I am a messenger. I am an Angel, though such a thing will not mean anything to you."

"An Angel! It is true I have never heard of such spirits. An Angel in white! I shall call you The White Angel!"

"Very well if you so wish," the Angel said with a smile upon his face.

"For whom is this message intended?" Nicholas then asked.

"It is a message for all humankind," replied the Angel, "though I fear that not all will listen. On this matter, that is all I will say. However my purpose is to visit certain people who have been chosen to hear first of what is taking place this night."

Nicholas was the type of person who liked to listen, so he was happy to oblige the White Angel. "I will listen," Nicholas said, keenly.

"Yes, you will listen. This I expected. But what of your fellow men and women? How many of them will take note of the good news that I bring? This, however, is the way of things, is it not?"

It was a rhetorical question, and the Angel continued, not wanting an answer.

"Humankind have within them the capacity to choose. They live their lives, as they think fit. Alas there are some who are drawn towards the ways of the Earth Spirit that you have so recently exchanged words with. As long as he has sway in the world, he will endeavour to make this so, ceaselessly seeking to draw more people towards his dark ways. Concern for people; this he never shows."

"Yes," interrupted Nicholas. "I thought him somewhat selfish and heartless. He did not seem to care about me, or anyone else for that matter. I can see now that he was also responsible for what followed, just after I left him."

"Ah yes the attack by the wolves," the Angel stated, indicating that he was aware of what had taken place.

Nicholas was quiet for a moment, recalling the near disastrous event. Then he looked at the White Angel.

"I will never forget what happened," Nicholas said ruefully. "It was a mistake. I should never have gone back, but I was curious how it could be that someone could just disappear. I wanted to check if there were any marks in the snow where the old man had been seated. All I found was the disturbances that I had created. That's when the wolves came. Fierce, hungry and determined they were. Never have I seen wolves so behave and they were nearly the end of me, but I managed to make it back to my sleigh. But that was more down to luck than skill."

"Yes. Luck often plays its part in such circumstances. Perhaps someone was protecting you, ensuring that you did survive," the Angel suggested.

This thought had not occurred to Nicholas, but on hearing the White Angel's words, he reflected a moment upon the notion.

But the White Angel did not want Nicholas to dwell on this, for he had more to reveal, so continuing, the Angel said, "What happened to you fits with the ways of the old man, the Earth Spirit, for I know his methods very well indeed."

"He did not seem to like you much," interjected Nicholas.

"Like me? What did he say about me?" asked the Angel.

"Not much, just that he intimated that you were responsible for reducing his influence over humankind, that you were driving him out of the world."

"Um! This is true in part," the Angel said in response.

"I don't think that he wanted me to meet you," Nicholas told the White Angel. "He told me a number of times to turn back and to return home."

"Yes, he would have tried to persuade you not to continue with your journey. When he saw that his powers of persuasion were not working on you, when he realised that he had no influence over you, in desperation he set the wolves on you."

"Set the wolves on me!" said a very surprised Nicholas. "Then he tried to kill me?"

"Yes, I am sure of it!" responded the Angel.

"Our meeting then, was no chance encounter?"

"Of that there can be no doubt," returned the Angel. "In revealing himself to you he had his purpose, just as I do. He knew that I intended to appear to you, and he tried to stop you reaching me. Even now he may be working to hinder you from completing your journey, which brings me to my message. You see, when he spoke to you, it was not me that he was referring to."

The White Angel paused, allowing Nicholas a few moments to wonder about what was coming next.

"You too then appear not by accident, but by design?"

"Yes," the Angel firmly stated.

"But why me?" Nicholas enquired. "Why do you choose to appear to me?"

"That is simple, my friend," the Angel began. "There is no-one more suited than you. You that have shown so much compassion, not just to your fellow men and women, but also to the wild creatures of the Earth. You that are loved so much by children. You that are so highly regard by all who know you."

Nicholas being a modest person found all this praise embarrassing and sought to stop the White Angel from saying anymore on the subject by directing his attention away towards other matters.

"So you have a purpose in appearing to me. Tell me what that purpose is. And if it was not you that the Earth Spirit was referring to, then whom was he talking about?"

So keen was Nicholas to change the subject of their conversation that he had for the moment quite forgotten himself, and was almost demanding answers from the White Angel, impatient as Nicholas was for more information and not to hear anymore said concerning himself.

"Patience my friend. All will be revealed. A purpose! Yes, I do have a purpose in appearing to you, and now it is time to tell you what brings me to you, here, on this special night. I am, my friend, as I have already told you, nothing more than a messenger. I am a herald of good tidings. I came into the world to tell people of the joyous event that is taking place, for tonight marks the beginning of a new age. The Earth Spirit, he that has dominated the world, spirit of the past as he is, complains for he knows that his time is over. His age is drawing to a close and a new one is dawning. What comes to pass this night will change the world forever! Of course, he resists, but it is futile to do so, for what is happening is far more powerful than he ever was, or will ever be."

There was an air of mystery and enchantment about the White Angel as he spoke these words. Nicholas' encounter with the Angel was unusual to be sure, but there was nothing in it that made him feel uneasy, unlike that which he had experienced with the old man, the Earth Spirit. Nicholas, utterly captivated and spellbound, sat listening to the words so eloquently spoken by this visitor from another realm. The utterance of these words left

Nicholas with a warm inner glow and he did not want the White Angel to stop speaking. He could have sat there for eternity, listening, at peace with himself, happy, joyous, and content. That the words should continue weaving their spell was all he wanted, and for the moment he had his wish, for the message that the Angel had brought did continue to flow from the youthful stranger's lips.

"No more will humankind dwell in the eternal darkness," the Angel said. "No more will humankind need to live a hopeless existence. For those that believe will find new hope and new life. This is the message that I bring here tonight. Cast off the past, look to future, for when tomorrow dawns it will be a different and better world that greets the rising sun. And behold look!"

As the Angel said these final words he looked straight at Nicholas, unfolding and raising his left arm until it was parallel to the snow covered ground, with his index finger pointing further along the road that Nicholas was travelling on his way to collect his Yule Log. The White Angel was inviting Nicholas to look, and he did. What did Nicholas observe?

Nicholas turned his head to see what the White Angel was pointing at, but was surprised for he could identify nothing unusual or special that was worth the Angel gesturing so.

Nicholas turned back to the Angel and asked, "To what do

you point? I see nothing out of the ordinary."

"Look again. Look harder this time," was the Angel's response.

So Nicholas did look one more time. Still nothing! But wait, perhaps there was something. Yes! It was a growing darkness that slowly and steadily developed into total blackness. There was no light at all. Where there had once been the dimness of the night, which is never completely unlit in a snow clad landscape, there was an abnormal darkness. It was disconcerting and it frightened Nicholas. He felt a tingling sensation run up his spine. Here was evil. Here was something unnatural.

Puzzled and alarmed Nicholas turned to the White Angel and spoke. "I only see an unnatural blackness the likes of which I have never seen before. What am I looking at?"

"What you see is absolute darkness. It is the nightfall of eternity. It is the blackness that comes with the dusk at the end of human existence. What you see is the ultimate fate of humankind if they do not change, if they continue to live as they have done in the past. But this fate is not inevitable. There is hope for salvation, and this hope enters your world tonight, far away, in another land, even stranger than this one. This hope comes in the form of a child born of simple folk. He will grow up to become a leader of souls, the Saviour of humanity. In Him many will find the peace that all humans, deep, deep within them crave. He will, through his words and deeds, inspire people to build a new world, one free from disease, suffering, discrimination, hatred, and wars. Through Him the lost souls of the human race will find their way back to where they belong, from where they originate, the source of all that is in the universe, and that which is the universe."

Of what the White Angel spoke, Nicholas did not fully comprehend. However Nicholas found it all most appealing, and would have spent his time engrossed in the thoughts that the vision stirred in him, if it had not been for the Angel's insistence that he focus his attention on what lay down the road.

"Now my friend I have spoken to you of the good news that I bring. This message I have delivered many times this night, but there is more for you than just words. Please look one more time. Cast your sight in the direction in which I point. Look again for I have things to show you that are only for your eyes. None I have visited have I shown what you are about to see. Be patient, take your time, look longer," the Angel said softly. "Look and behold what is happening."

So Nicholas turned once more and gazed upon the darkness that had fallen upon the land some distance along the forest track. Again there was nothing but that frightening blackness which had engulfed a small part of the frozen world that Nicholas was so familiar with, which now no more could be seen. It was as if some unearthly force had swallowed it up. Then, a startling event began to unfold!

High up in the heavens, among the pinpricks of twinkling lights that were the stars, a tiny light appeared, faint at first, but increasing in its intensity as every second passed. It grew until it glowed large and bright—a new star had formed, bursting into life with an explosion of luminance that lit up the world in a way that has never been witnessed before, and will never be seen again! Shining brilliantly in the sky above, it was as though the darkness of the night was no more. Far down below, it seemed as though all this star's intensity were directed at one point upon the Earth. Some way along the road he had yet to travel, one spot was singled out. There, in the distance, there was a sight worth seeing.

Now this place was some way off, so the detail was not fully evident to Nicholas. It appeared to him that there were a number of people, gathered together, and it seemed as though they were gazing down, as if there was some item or person that was worth the long attention that they paid it. What it could be Nicholas had no idea, but the light from the new star seemed to be most intense upon that spot, which did itself also glow as if a piece of this celestial body had fallen to Earth, and at that place it did lie and radiate light.

Nicholas also noted that it was as though the unnatural darkness that had befallen the land did retreat before this wondrous light as if it had no right to be there in the presence of such purity.

Nicholas rose to his feet, mesmerised by what he was witnessing, still gazing at the scene before him.

"You have seen it?" the Angel gently asked, not wanting to disturb Nicholas, who seemed to be lost in the wonder of what he was observing.

"I have seen something, but what it is I am not sure," Nicholas replied. Then, with some difficulty he turned to the White Angel, for to be truthful, Nicholas did not want to look away least the scene disappear and be lost to his sight forever.

"What is it?" Nicholas asked the White Angel in astonishment.

"What it is, is what I have told you about," was the Angel's initial reply. Then he added, "But the details you must discover for yourself, for it is given to you on this night, among all men, the opportunity to be a witness of the wondrous event now unfolding. You must take your leave of me and follow the road that will bring you to where those people stand, and there discover your destiny."

Nicholas had once more turned his eyes towards the light that shone in the darkness. But on hearing the White Angel mention the word destiny, he turned once again towards him and asked,

"My destiny? What are you talking about?"

"Questions! Always more questions," the Angel said smiling. "I cannot tell you all that you need to know. There are some things in life that you need to discover for yourself. The only way to do that is to make the journey. Go and see for yourself what lies along the road. Discovery is part of what life is about. It's a gift that you humans have been given—the chance to explore and learn. Use this gift now. There is nothing to fear."

Nicholas understood that he would never discover what lay ahead, what was happening, if he did not do as the White Angel urged. Deep inside he knew what his next step would be. There, along the track, was the place where he now had to head. Caught up in the events of that night, there was no thought of going home. Whatever was waiting for him, it was not to be ignored. It was as if it were calling to him, compelling him to come and see for himself the sight upon which the small group did stare.

Nicholas faced the White Angel for the last time. The Angel was still smiling at him.

"I will go, for I see that this is where events are directing me," Nicholas told him.

"Good," the Angel replied. "Then my work here is done."

"Will you not come with me?" Nicholas enquired.

"Alas I cannot. I came here to deliver a message to you, to

reveal to you the events of the night, and that task is now completed. My time in this world is finished. Over! Go now to your sleigh, with its bright red panels, for to stay here once I have left is to invite those wolves to come for you again, and that I cannot allow, but my energy, my will to hold on to this material world is already beginning to fade. Hurry! Hurry! On your way! Be gone!"

There was an urgency in the White Angel's final words that was not lost on Nicholas, who now looked for one last time at the Angel who, in a few short minutes, had become a dear friend. No more would Nicholas see him, no more would they speak. For in an instance the Angel would be as though he had never been. Back to his heavenly world he would retreat, leaving Nicholas vulnerable to the perils of his own.

Nicholas had learnt his lesson from the encounter with the Earth Spirit. There would be danger once the Angel had departed, and he would not stay to see him go. Pressing on, continuing with his journey, heading for the scene that lay along the road— this now was all Nicholas wanted to do. So with a grateful heart he bid the White Angel farewell, and was, in a moment, back in his sleigh, heading away.

With oil lights aglow, bells gently jingling, and torches flaming in the darkness, racing through the night, no time to dally, or to ponder and weigh, Nicholas continued on his way. On through the darkness his reindeer did lead, towards the light that was beckoning him near.

So it was, for the third time that night, Nicholas drew up his sleigh, for beside the road was a most wondrous sight, far more mysterious than anything he had experienced in the first two encounters of the night.

CHAPTER FOUR

FATHER CHRISTMAS

It was neither very close nor very far from the location where Nicholas had met the White Angel, to the spot illuminated by the bright star. He had journeyed along the road towards this place, half expecting trouble, for the words of the Angel concerning the Earth Spirit had haunted him, even though feelings of peace and joy were still fresh in his mind—emotions which came from hearing joyous news and from observing wondrous events. But the Earth Spirit did not bother Nicholas again and his journey proved to be uneventful.

Shortly after leaving the White Angel Nicholas noticed again that the wolves had returned, once more shadowing him along the way, until his safe arrival, when for the third time, they hid in the forest with eyes keenly set on the human gathering. In the course of his travelling, full as it was of anticipation, Nicholas did not have cause for concern about the resumed presence of the wild creatures that seemed set upon dogging his journey that night. On the contrary, Nicholas had become resigned to their presence, assuming now that they too had some part to play in the night's events.

Amazed, enchanted, and captivated was Nicholas at the sight that greeted him, observing it for the moment from the side of the track, not ready at this point to approach the assembly. Nicholas did not step forward for some time, but stayed in the sleigh for what seemed to him an age. In truth however it may have only been a few seconds, for time that night had lost all meaning.

Set by the side of the road was a scene in many ways bizarre, but nevertheless enthralling, and Nicholas just stared at it, taking it all in, absorbing the atmosphere, noting the details, looking closely at what he saw, trying to make some sense of it.

Before him were several people wearing strange and unfamiliar clothes. Most were plainly dressed, but three stood out from the rest, being attired in grand and colourful robes, decorated with silver and gold material that glittered and sparkled in the light cast by the flickering flames of the warm fire that burnt to one side of the group. These three men were indeed regal looking persons and had about them the air of noblemen. In their hands they held small boxes, lids open. Nicholas could not make out what these boxes contained, but given the bearers' evident wealth, precious items seemed the most obvious contents.

As for the others, three of them were no more than young boys all of whom were dressed in plain clothes and each wore a sheepskin coat. They, in contrast to the first three Nicholas had observed, were unmistakably poor, and had nothing to offer in the way of gifts. This however did not seem to matter, for the boys were well pleased to be present, and no-one thought any the worse of them for not having any offerings. With these young boys were animals that Nicholas recognised as sheep, though in Nicholas' cold and frozen land they did not dwell, but having journeyed one time southwards to warmer, sunnier lands, Nicholas did recognise them as such. From this Nicholas surmised that the boys must be shepherds.

With the sheep, there also stood some cattle. One other creature Nicholas also knew; it was a donkey. All these animals were quiet—not a single sound did any of the creatures make. Then, as he watched this spectacle, Nicholas was surprised to see the wolves come out from their forest retreat—the same ones that had followed him all along his journey, the same ones that had nearly made a meal of him.

Now, previously mentioned in this story, was the observation that these wild and ferocious creatures would that night meet their match. This is the point where this happened. Leaving the shelter of the trees and trotting across the snow, were not the fierce and dangerous beasts of the forest that Nicholas knew and feared, but mild and timid creatures. They sat down upon the snow, near to the sheep, looking on at the gathering, not as prey as is their want, but as though like well mannered pet dogs waiting patiently for their master.

All the people that Nicholas observed were assembled in a group, and not on snow they stood, but on straw as if in a barn or a stable. In the midst of this gathering was a couple, husband and wife, Nicholas assumed, who sat by a manger full of straw, the woman holding an infant child, and these two people and their new born baby were at the centre of everyone's attention.

What can be said concerning these new parents, this man and woman? Very little, for a more plain a pair one would be hard pushed to find. Dressed in the clothes of poor peasant types, with little in the way of personal possessions, neither of them had any features that were in anyway remarkable or worthy of comment. They were neither very beautiful, nor very ugly. They were people that one would pass by without a second thought or glance. Altogether there was nothing connected with them that suggested any reason why the gathered observers should stare in wonderment at them, except perhaps for one thing—the new born baby wrapped in plain white cloth and held by its mother in her arms. It was upon this baby that the starlight from high up above shone down. It was as if the star had been created just for this child, to light up its world so that all that wished to look upon it could see the innocent babe.

Nicholas, with his eyes set upon this picture of adoration, recalled what the youthful stranger, the White Angel, had told to him, but so far Nicholas only partially comprehended what was taking place. Here must be the Saviour of which the Angel had spoken, this baby, so small, and still so new to the world—this innocent infant must be He.

Glancing upwards Nicholas could see the star shining down upon the place were these people had come, its light falling upon the new born baby so soft and fair. The people gathered there, dressed as they were in such a peculiar way, had a look about them that was, without doubt, to be that of a far, far distant land. All spoke in a strange tongue, and the words they uttered were incompressible to Nicholas' ears. The language strange and unknown left Nicholas wondering what they were saying. Then, and not for the first time that night as will soon become clear, a small miracle happened. For Nicholas this could be said to be the beginning.

At first Nicholas did not sense it. All seemed as it had been. It grew upon him slowly, creeping up stealthily, like a tiger stalking its prey. At first there was the occasional flickering of perception, of understanding, but for the most part the words that the people spoke were as they had been for the length of time that Nicholas had first heard them—all strange and alien. Most of what they said was as meaningless as if Nicholas had not heard at all because of some affliction with his hearing, but little by little more of the words started to make sense. The people still spoke their strange language, but Nicholas began to comprehend what they were saying. He did not know how this was so, but pieces of their conversation slowly became discernible, until at last all that was spoken was as clear to Nicholas as if it had been stated in his own tongue.

This was a gift given to Nicholas that night, one that he would never lose, and which, in the course of time, would come to be very useful. Over the many years that were to follow that special and mysterious night, with all its magical encounters, Nicholas had many occasions to use this precious gift. Why you ask? The reason will become clear as this story draws to its close.

Nicholas listened to what the gathered people said and pieced together the story of the folk that stood before him.

First, one of the young shepherds spoke.

"A young man dressed in white suddenly appeared from nowhere," the shepherd said.

Nicholas immediately recognised this person of which the shepherd spoke as the White Angel he had himself encountered not too long past.

"We were very frightened at first," the shepherd continued. "But the stranger reassured us and said he was an Angel and that no harm would come to us. And then we all felt calm, as if by magic. The Angel then spoke of the birth of a King and that we should visit a stable in the nearby town of Bethlehem, which we did, bringing with us our sheep and lambs."

Then one of the noblemen spoke.

"Our tale is also a mysterious one," he began. "We have, for many months, read the signs in the night sky. Eventually, after much observation and discussion, we concluded that these were a portent of the coming of a new King that would be King of Kings. We thought it wise therefore to seek out this new King. So we set out many moons ago, searching for Him so that we could pay homage to this new ruler. Long have we travelled, not sure of where exactly we were headed, but steered, it seems to us, in the right direction by some unseen helping hand. Then, suddenly, a new and bright star appeared in the sky nearby the place where we were camped, and this star guided us here, where we are now all assembled."

All the visitors spoke of this baby in the most reverend tone.

They said that He was the Son of God, that He had come into the world to save humanity, and that He was their Saviour.

Now at this point Nicholas became lost, for he knew nothing of God. What was God? The only gods that Nicholas knew of were the those of the elements that ruled over his life, in the cold and harsh world in which he lived—the gods of fire, earth, water, wind, snow and ice. These were the deities that his people worshipped. No-one had ever said anything about a God, singular.

Nicholas looked on, separate from the scene being played out before him, listening in, and learning about what it was that was unfolding that night to which he and the others were witnesses. So it was that the full story became clear. Based on what the White Angel had told Nicholas, what Nicholas had seen when the new star burst into life, and the tales that the gathered people had told, Nicholas for the most part, in the end, did understand. Now at last, all but one thing, God, made sense. Concerning this God Nicholas still wondered, asking himself what this could be, for he did not know of God, this concept which no-one in his world had ever before encountered.

As ever, a helping hand was there to guide Nicholas. It came in the form of a wonderful occurrence, which happened rather suddenly. Out of the blue, a feeling of calm and peace swept over Nicholas, and elevated him into a state of mind that was pure elation. It was as if the worries, cares and pains of the world had been lifted from him. At that point Nicholas left his sleigh, as though invited to do so, and he walked forward towards those assembled, who made a space for him as he approached, revealing as they did so the baby, who, so it seemed to Nicholas, was gazing right at him.

Soon Nicholas was among the gathered visitors. He dressed for the cold of the far north and they attired for some much warmer land far away. He with his long cloak of green, trimmed along the edges with the fur of the white fox, his fur lined trousers and large brown snow boots, and they with their lighter clothes, regal and royal in the case of the noblemen, plain and functional for the rest. How out of keeping with them Nicholas looked, but no-one cared. He was made as welcome as the poorest among them. No-one queried Nicholas' presence. Everyone had a right to be there, all had been invited, and for the moment they were all equal. No-one among them held any rank in the presence of this holy infant.

Then Nicholas heard it. A voice in the night, soft and quiet at first, then growing until it became clear to him. It spoke to him and to him only, for none of the others gave any sign that they too could hear. It was not like the voice of a human, consisting of the sounds of words, but something far more mystical and heavenly, communicating with Nicholas, as if planting within his mind the seeds of understanding, that grew and burst into awareness and knowledge. No, when Nicholas had first arrived and listened to what was said, he had not known about the God of which they spoke. He knew nothing of God, or the Son of God, but in a flash Nicholas knew. All was revealed to him. It was like a bolt of lighting striking him, filling him with life and energy and love. He knew. How he came to know, the mechanics of this transference, of the revelation, he could not fully say and this did not bother him at all, for Nicholas did not care. It did not matter how, he just knew, and he fell down on his knees full of gladness and humility.

But that was not the end of it. Concerning God Nicholas was now aquatinted, but the voice had not finished with him, for it had more to tell. So the communication continued, speaking to Nicholas of things that must be. Nicholas listened and was happier than he had ever been. It was of course the baby that was the source of all this, although no sounds did it make. Then the message given to Nicholas changed, for within it now were many instructions. What to do and how! These filled his mind creating visions of what would be, made so by His will.

Then, just as suddenly as it had begun, when all was told, the communication ceased. Nicholas was still kneeling, but immediately rose to his feet and stood looking at the sight before him, feeling quite different from previously. There were aspects to him that had altered. Nicholas knew this, but what exactly had changed? Nicholas seemed to be, by the moment, undergoing a metamorphous, not just mentally but also physically, transforming into a different person.

Standing, observing, feeling the alterations taking place, little by little he began to notice the changes. First his clothes. As if by magic his lovely green hooded cloak, trimmed along the edges with the fur of the white fox, had changed colour. No more was it the spruce green that is was, but now a magnificent bright red, and the trimming was whiter than white. His trousers and tunic had also become bright red, and his brown snow boots were now as black as coal. His thick beard, once short had become much longer, and not a trace of colour was left in it. Like the hair on his head, both were white as virgin snow. What is more, he saw that he had grown a little around his waist, but his clothes still fitted him perfectly.

Inside, in his mind, Nicholas was also feeling different as well. All worries and concerns had left him. He was peaceful, calm and content. Much more however, for he was feeling jolly and merry, and quite suddenly he let out a laugh, "Ho, ho, ho!" he said, with great surprise.

Looking once more at the new born child, Nicholas' heart was filled with a yearning to act. It came upon him, and made him smile, as if in his mind's eye Nicholas could see it all.

With a nod and a wink to the baby, Nicholas said, "I'll be away. It's time."

Then Nicholas turned quickly and headed back to his sleigh. And here too there were changes. To his eye it seemed much the same, still painted bright red, just like the colour of his clothes, except in the luggage space, which had before been quite empty, there was now a pile of bright red sacks, each bulging with little parcels. Nicholas knew exactly what these were for.

There was however also a subtler difference about the sleigh that did not affect the way it looked. Yes, this was his sleigh, old and familiar to him, but it had an air about it as if it had a life of its own. It almost pulsed with energy, and immediately Nicholas knew why and was filled with the delight of a child taking its first sleigh ride.

Mounting the sleigh and seated once more, Nicholas made himself cosy. Comfortable and warm under the furs that had lain unused so far that night, he shouted at the reindeer.

"Ya!" Nicholas said, and they were on their way. At first across snow on the ground they did slide, as before, but not for long, for as soon as they were underway, up into the air they began to climb. High up into the starry heavens they flew, until they were but a small speck passing across the sky. Nicholas looked down as if to bid farewell, but already the scene had faded far away.

Now all this did not frighten Nicholas, nor was he surprised, for what had transpired was exactly what he had been told. He knew also that up there, oh so high, he was quite safe, and that no mishaps would befall him.

From his vantage point up above the sleeping world, Nicholas saw tiny points of light glowing in the darkness down below and recognised immediately what they were and smiled. These he would see year after year, being the souls of every living child, innocently sleeping, waiting for the new day.

Many children were awoken that strange first Christmas night by a mysterious notion that crept into their minds, that each and every one would be blessed before the coming dawn, by a new visitor who would bring with him presents—gifts of toys and sweet things to eat. Looking out from their bedroom windows they gazed, wondering and waiting, anticipating the delight!

Visiting every single child in the world that night, delivering gifts, Nicholas circled the globe in his flying sleigh. Shooting across the sky, his reindeer effortlessly galloping through the air, it was a sight to behold with its oil lights aglow, bells gently jingling, and torches flaming in the darkness. This spectacle, all children in every land and in every generation, would come to know.

When it was all over, when the happiness had been given in equal measure, not to his home did Nicholas then return, but to a new dwelling in a secret place. Far into the land of the great white bear, close to the North Pole, did his flying sleigh take him, into a palace of ice hidden from human sight.

Although on the outside it was cold and hard, deep inside there was a warming glow, and here Nicholas dwelt forever more, knowing that he, once every year, was privileged among humankind to bring happiness into the lives of every single child that would ever exist. Even some adults, at least those not miserable and grumpy and inclined to forget, could if they so wished on Christmas Eve, partake in the magic and experience again the childish excitement and joy, once taken for granted, of Father Christmas' extraordinary flight.

~

Next day at Nicholas' house, his friends gathered as had been arranged, but soon found that their host was not at home. Alarmed and concerned they searched around close by and soon discovered that the sleigh and reindeer were gone. The tracks leading south into the forest they next discovered. Aware of Nicholas' plans to bring home the Yule Log that night just gone, they began to fear the worst and set off to find their dear friend. Using their own sleigh they followed Nicholas' trail, until they spied the place where Nicholas had first halted to speak with the Earth Spirit.

The footsteps in the snow they observed which puzzled them somewhat for they seemed to lead to nothing. On seeing the wolf prints in the snow however, they began to fear for their missing friend. But on discovering no sign of blood on the ground, and marks left by the sleigh's runners that continued along the road, they were relieved to learn that, there at least, Nicholas had not fallen fowl of that dangerous pack.

Proceeding onward the second spot they soon did find. Again they were bemused by Nicholas' strange behaviour in leaving the safety of his sleigh to stand at the roadside. Then they saw that the sleigh tracks in the road did still lead on. So with hope in their hearts they journeyed further along the road till, for a third time, they stopped to wonder why Nicholas had once again halted and stood by the road.

All was a mystery to them, so to follow more sleigh marks in the snow they continued their journey along the way, but came quickly to a halt on seeing that no further tracks could be seen. They hunted around, walking further along to see if there was any sign of Nicholas and his sleigh, but nothing did they find.

Now perplexed, they concluded that a terrible mishap had befallen their friend. Being simple folk, superstitious in nature, they imagined that Nicholas had been carried off by some large winged creature, taken and eaten, and his remains left for scavengers to finish off. So they searched for his body, visiting the place where Nicholas had prepared his Yule Log, perhaps in a vain hope that he might be there, waiting patiently for them to come and rescue him. They eventually found the log, but no sign of Nicholas there was. Thus with heavy hearts they gave up their search and turned and set off home, now sure that Nicholas was no more.

But this, as all children know, was not how it was. Far away, in a place close to the North Pole, Nicholas listened to the children's voices that he heard in his head, spoken in the many languages of the Earth, but understood regardless of this. Thus knowing each child's heartfelt wish, twelve months did pass, and one year on to the very night, Nicholas on his sleigh did once more streak across the sky, bringing happiness to an expectant world. Racing across the starry heavens with oil lights aglow, bells gently jingling, and torches flaming in the darkness, he brought joy wherever he went. Around the globe Nicholas did travel, all in one night, delivering gifts to expectant children, bringing childish delight into millions of lives.

So it has been ever since that first Christmas night. Across the ages, in good times and bad, through famine and feast, in war and in peace, Nicholas, Father Christmas, now more often called Santa Claus, goes about the task that was given to him one Yuletide Eve, long, long ago, in a far away place, deep inside the frozen lands of the north, close to where the vast coniferous forests that are the habitat of the wild brown bear, gives way to the treeless domain of the great white bear. There, in a time before time, before the world was full of clocks that measure the slipping away of every fleeting second, before there were any calendars to reckon the passing of the days, when there was no need for such things, and the passage of time was noted by the turning of the seasons, extraordinary events did unfold. There, in this now distant and long forgotten world, Father Christmas made his first appearance and the magic of Christmas began. And now you know how Father Christmas came to be. Merry Christmas!

The End